T
Glass
Bird

Books by the same author

The Time Tree

For older readers

My Mother's Daughter
The Game

The Glass Bird

Enid Richemont

Illustrations by
Caroline Anstey

WALKER BOOKS
LONDON

For Jeremy, with love

First published 1990 by Walker Books Ltd
87 Vauxhall Walk, London SE11 5HJ

First printed 1990
Printed and bound in Great Britain by
Richard Clay Ltd, Bungay, Suffolk

British Library Cataloguing in Publication Data
Richemont, Enid
The glass bird.
I. Title
823'.914 [F]

ISBN 0-7445-1903-9
ISBN 0-7445-1730-3 Pbk

CONTENTS

Chapter One

Adam was lonely.

He knew plenty of people. He had a mother and a father. He had aunts and uncles. He had two grannies and a grandpa who sometimes gave him presents, but anyone could have had those things. A brother or a sister might have been nice but his mum was always saying: "One is more than enough."

A friend was what Adam really wanted.

A friend was something special.

It wasn't that anyone disliked Adam, although sometimes, they did tease him because he wouldn't fight.

He'd tried to explain it to people.

“We’re Quakers,” he would say. “It’s a kind of religion.” But that only made them giggle and ask: “What you do then – quake?”

So he stopped saying it.

Fighting wasn’t a problem anyway. Fighting was stupid. Who wanted to fight?

The problem was that, when they weren’t teasing him, nobody noticed him. Other people went round in gangs. Other people had friends. Some people had best friends. Adam had no one.

Most of the time, he pretended it didn’t matter.

He was pretending hard when he came out of the playground on that late October afternoon. Boys jostled past him, searching for conkers, or pelting each other with armfuls of dead leaves. Adam longed to join in, but he didn’t know how.

He found himself a conker, anyway. He liked conkers, and this was a particularly good one. He scrubbed it against his sleeve, admiring the golden water patterns on its glossy surface. At the bus stop some kids from his class were fooling about. He glanced at them, trying to think of something funny to say, but the words just wouldn't come.

Words in Adam's mouth never seemed to sound right. One reason, he knew, was that everybody else could talk about the things

they'd watched on television, and his family didn't even have one. "There are much better things to spend money on," his dad said. "You'll be grateful one day."

But Adam didn't want to be grateful one day. Adam loved his mum and dad but oh, how he wished they could be a bit more like other people's.

Wishes, he thought scornfully. Kids' stuff. Fairy godmothers and magic apples – daft! In those old stories, anything could turn out to be magic – fishes, buttons, even the conker he was holding in his hand. Daft! Silly! Stupid.

But if magic were true, a conker would be as good as anything else. He thought about it as he walked up the High Street. Magic conkers? Ha, ha! That was a joke. But if it were magic, what could it do? Give you wishes, of course, dumb-dumb – what else?

Well, supposing it gave you three wishes.

OK, so pretend.

Now watch it, he told himself; you've got to be careful with wishes or they go all wrong...

Well, then: Wish Number One – a telly. Of his own. A secret one. In his room. Colour, of course, and big. Huge. A super-enormous telly with remote controls (remote controls were great. Pow! and you could change channels! Pow! Pow!) And a video. And a Space Invaders game (did that count as three things already?).

But wow! With that lot, everyone would want to know him. Kids would be queuing up to be asked back to his place. He'd have to be choosy – one or two of them were wreckers and couldn't be trusted – but some were really nice, like Mike, who lived on a farm, or Gary, whose dad kept racing pigeons (how did you get a pigeon to race?).

He kicked at a can and sent it spinning into the gutter. He might win a telly, he supposed. In one of those raffle things. Better to do it that way. The trouble with wishes – there was always a catch. You had to be clever and choose the right words.

All the same...

Money, he thought; now that was a good one. You couldn't go wrong with money. Loads of money. Billions of pounds.

Well, OK. Money could be his second wish.

The first wish was the important one.

He cancelled the telly. After all, when he was rich, he could buy hundreds.

It was friends he wanted.

He turned into the small stretch of country road on the edge of the common. There was no one to hear, so why not? It was silly, of course, but it was only pretend. He held the conker tightly and closed his eyes.

"I wish," he said (feeling a bit silly), "that I had friends. A whole lot of friends." He paused. Was that being greedy? He corrected himself hastily. "Well just one would do."

And into that warm and windless afternoon, there came a sudden breeze. It puffed into his face like a big breath, and then whirled lightly over the common, rustling the stalks of the dried-up ferns.

Then everything was still again.

Chapter Two

Somebody called out: “Hello, Adam!”

It worked, thought Adam joyfully. I didn’t believe it was magic but it was and it worked, and he opened his eyes.

“Want a lift home?”

It was his teacher.

Not someone from his class who was having second thoughts about him, but only his teacher, his rotten old teacher in her rotten old car.

She smiled at him.

“I’m going right past your house today, Adam. Want a lift?”

Adam felt his face growing hot with

embarrassment. All that "magic" stuff – had she seen? Had she heard?

"No, thanks," he managed to say. "I'm sort of – waiting for a friend."

Some magic, he thought crossly, as her car moved off. Stupid. Couldn't it tell the difference? It was not that he didn't like Miss Thomas – she wasn't all that bad – but a teacher couldn't be a friend.

Caught out by his silly pretend game, he hurled the conker away. It hit a clump of ferns. He watched them crackle and shake, and felt a bit better. Wow, he thought; not a bad throw; not bad at all.

But the funny thing was, the ferns went on shaking, as if the wind were still blowing but only in one place.

He tried to work it out. It could be some small animal – a rabbit, perhaps: there were plenty of those on the common. Once he had even seen a fox. He liked foxes. He liked guinea-pigs and gerbils. He liked lots of animals, and the only thing his family had was a boring old cat.

He decided to track whatever it was. Crouching, he moved stealthily through the grass, ducking from time to time and watching the ferns for any sudden movement. Warily, he crept right up to them. There was still nothing – only a funny glittery thing half-hidden by leaves. Glass, probably, caught in the sunlight, or a tin can, or an old bottle; nothing interesting, nothing alive. The ferns were quite still now; the animal, or whatever it was, had long since fled, but Adam was still curious. He crawled up to the shining place and gently parted the brittle stems.

And then he could not move. He could not even blink. All he could do was stare and stare.

It was the most beautiful thing he had ever seen, and he knew that he would remember it for the rest of his life. He couldn't be sure whether it was still pretend, or whether he was dreaming: was it possible to dream while you were still awake and walking around?

He shook himself and looked away, blinking, but when he looked back, it was still the same.

Down there, deep among the ferns, stood a bird. It wasn't very big – about the same size as a very large pigeon, but you can forget about pigeons.

This bird was made of glass.

Its back and its wings were covered in

bright, glassy scales, and from the centre of each scale a tinselly down grew outward in a star pattern that seemed to twinkle and spin. The shafts of the feathers were luminous and glowing, as if they had been painted with a brush dipped in light, and as they moved upward into the neck, they grew smaller and finer until they turned into glittering threads of bright crystal.

And as the scales and feathers changed their direction, they mirrored all the brown and green and gold of the grasses and ferns, and sometimes (and most wonderful of all) caught the light of the sun and splintered it into a thousand shimmering rainbows.

Adam held his breath. Somebody, he thought at last, must have made this thing. A very special somebody: an artist, perhaps. Maybe it had come from one of the posh houses up on the hill. Maybe someone had stolen it. A burglar. He glanced nervously round; the thief might be watching him. But there was no one in sight.

He turned back to the bird. Glass? He wasn't sure any more. What, then? Sequins? But where could you buy sequins as bright as that? Perhaps they were really bits of diamond. Adam had never seen a real diamond, but he knew that it couldn't be more glittery than this. What could be more glittery than those star-bright feathers, more shimmery than that silver web between its toes or more pearly than those funny toe-nails that shone like little crescent moons?

And the strangest thing of all was that the glittery stuff looked, not stuck, not stitched, but as if it were really growing there. Whoever had made it must have been very, very clever.

Adam wondered what to do. If he picked it up (but supposing he dropped it?) he could take it to the police station (but what if the burglar came sneaking up the road to pick up his loot?). Safer to leave it where it was, and go home and tell his mum.

Then the bird turned its head and looked at him.

"I am dreaming this," Adam told himself slowly. "I must have gone to sleep in the grass." He put out his hand and tested the ferns. They felt real enough. He patted the ground and his finger caught on a thorn – ouch! That felt real enough, and so was the small bead of blood on his fingertip. In the distance he could hear the hum of a tractor, and the church clock chiming half past four – could you hear things like that in a dream?

For a long time he crouched there, not moving. At last he put out a timid finger and touched the bird's body. It was hard and soft, cold and warm, all at the same time, like nothing he'd ever felt before. He touched its head, where the down curled softly round its cheeks, and gasped – Oooh! – when the bird suddenly stretched its wings and shook out its feathers with a soft, metallic fluttering.

Then, afraid that it might suddenly fly away and be lost to him for ever, he put out his hand.

"Oh please don't go," he begged.

And as if it had understood, the bird closed its wings and stepped up on to Adam's finger. "Stepped" is just what it did: like a person, it put first one foot forward and then the other, curling its strange, silvery toes round the side of Adam's hand.

Adam stood up shakily. The bird was surprisingly heavy, and the underneath of its body was ice-cold, not at all like something alive. Oh it wasn't true, he thought. It couldn't really be alive. Not like dogs and cats and rabbits. Not like him.

Then it shifted, moved, and he knew that it was.

It must, he decided, be somebody's pet. A very important Somebody. A very rich Somebody. It must be valuable; no one would just abandon it. Had it escaped? Had it been stolen? Did people steal rare animals? Of course they did, stupid.

Just then a car slowed down and stopped on the edge of the common. Adam ducked, and held his breath. He peered through the ferns. A fat woman opened the back door, and out tumbled three fussy small dogs, yapping furiously. Adam heard her calling them to heel, and watched them prancing around her, jumping and yelping, as she began striding across the grass.

He made up his mind. Dogs were risky. He had no choice. He couldn't leave the bird where it was: anything might happen to it.

Holding one side of his anorak protectively in front of it, Adam walked the rest of the way home.

Chapter Three

In the long grass at the bottom of Adam's large, untidy garden, next door's kitten was playing a stalking game. As Adam came in through the back gate, it sprang out – "Gotcher!" – and pounced on his trailing bootlaces. He would have laughed, and played with it, but now he couldn't. Cats hunted birds, didn't they? Horrified, he nudged the kitten with his toe and sent it tumbling over the grass. For a second it staggered, puzzled at finding itself somewhere else; then it wriggled and crouched for another spring.

Cats, thought Adam bitterly. That meant he

couldn't take the bird into the house: Mopsie might be old but she was still a good mouser. So where on earth could he put it? Where would it be safe?

He looked around. There was always the summer-house, he supposed.

Long ago the summer-house had been tucked neatly behind the curve of a smooth lawn, but now it was hidden behind hawthorn and brambles. Nobody ever sat in it, and it was much too rotten to store things in. The roof leaked, the windows had rusted shut, and the door hung from one hinge and would only stay closed if you jammed it with a stone. Recently his dad had started talking about taking an axe to it, now that they had a nice new garden shed. The only person who bothered with it was Adam. It was all right to muck about in. It made a good den, if he was in the mood.

He kicked away the stone and the door fell open. Not bad, he thought. Cat-proof, too, when it was properly closed up. He unloaded

his bird gently on to the dusty shelf. Among the spiders' webs and broken flowerpots and bits and pieces from forgotten games, it sparkled and shone like a king's crown. Adam caught his breath. What a wonder it was, and all his!

No, it wasn't. It belonged to someone, didn't it?

He gazed at it wistfully, looking and looking, because when it was gone, he wanted to remember. Now, through all the glitter, he could see places so glassy-clear that he could pick out the delicate outlines of the bird's skeleton. Adam gasped. It was scary and he didn't know what to do. Eight was pretty old, but right now he wished he were grown up.

Words formed inside his head: "Don't be afraid."

"So who's afraid?" said Adam crossly.

"Help," said the words. "I need your help."

Adam looked round, but no one was there. He stared back at the bird, but that was silly. Birds couldn't speak.

Not true, he remembered. Parrots could.

"Polly?" he tried. "Pretty Polly?"

The eyes flashed silver.

"You're wasting time."

Adam gulped.

"I'll be right back," he said. "I'll fetch my mum. She's great. She'll help. Don't you worry."

He closed the door, dragging up the stone. Then he ran back to the house.

"Mum!" he shouted. "Come and see what I've found!"

His mother came out of the kitchen.

"Hello, love. You're a bit late – had a good day?"

He smelt a cigarette, and his heart sank.

He didn't even have to look: he knew who was in there.

"We'll have some tea in a while with Auntie Sarah," his mum said vaguely, already edging into the sitting room. "But if you can't wait, there's a couple of sticky buns over there. Danish, with apple. Special treat." He heard her settling into the sofa. "So what happened after the committee meeting?" she was saying. Her voice sounded quite different – eager and enthusiastic.

Adam sighed, and went on up to his room. If he told his mum now, Aunt Sarah would have to be part of his secret, too, and that was something he didn't want. If Aunt Sarah saw his bird, it would lose some of its specialness. Aunt Sarah could take the magic out of anything.

He lay on his bed, making paper aeroplanes and crashing them gloomily against the walls until they called him down for tea.

Mum had set out pretty cups and saucers, and a mug of Ovaltine for Adam on the sitting-room table. She glanced up from her papers as he came in.

"What was it you wanted to show me?" she asked.

"Oh, nothing much."

He felt his face grow hot, as it always did when he was lying. Aunt Sarah noticed, and grinned.

"Guilty secrets already, young man?"

Adam stared down at his sticky bun and wished she'd go away. Some of his mum's friends he quite liked, but not this one. Aunt Sarah was always boasting about how she understood children. Well Adam didn't want to be understood.

The conversation moved back to things grown-up. Adam fidgeted and yawned and at last slipped away unnoticed into the back garden. After so much boredom, he was beginning to wonder if the bird had ever really existed, or if it had been some sort of super-pretend, but when he stepped into the summer-house, there it was, all dazzling, watching him with its strange, glittery eyes.

He put out a finger and touched its twinkly throat and its silvery wings. The pattern of the skeleton through the almost transparent body still scared him, and the faint flickering of several pulses reminded him uncomfortably that the bird was alive. Adam shivered. Cats he knew about, but not birds. Anyway, this was no ordinary bird – no blackbird nor starling nor thrush; not even a budgie. What kind of a creature was it? What did it live on? What did it need? Would his mother really know? Would his dad?

Once again, a word came into his head.

"Water."

Water? But he wasn't thirsty.

"Water. Yes. Give me water and I will live."

"Oh," said Adam. "For you. I get it. Yes. Water. OK."

He closed the door carefully and ran back to the house.

Chapter Four

In the kitchen Adam found Mopsie's drinking bowl. He scrubbed it and filled it with clean water. It was an old china bowl, once white with a blue stripe, but now the white was stained and covered with a network of fine cracks, and even though he had scrubbed it clean, it still looked grubby.

How could he bring his bird water in a thing like that?

He put it down and looked around. There was a glass ice-cream bowl but it was much too small, and anyway, you could buy things like that in Woolworths. No. He needed something special.

There was a cupboard where his mother kept a small collection of old china and glass. Suddenly he knew exactly what he wanted.

He opened the cupboard and reached up carefully for the swan bowl. He set it down on the table and looked at it with satisfaction. It was a heavy, cut-glass bowl shaped like a swan, and it had belonged to his mother's granny. They used it now on special occasions, like Christmas or birthdays, filling its back with nuts or sweets. A glass bird to carry water to a glass bird – now that was really special. And his mum wouldn't mind, once he'd explained...

He filled a jug with water, not trusting himself to carry the swan bowl over to the tap in case he chipped it on the hard edge of the sink. Then, with great concentration, he walked slowly out to the garden. The bowl was quite heavy now, and as he moved, the water slopped from side to side, wetting the tips of his fingers. He watched it, fascinated, proud of his balance and control.

A tornado of fur and claws shot between his feet, as next door's kitten fled from a furious Mopsie. Adam stepped on Mopsie's tail. She shrieked. Startled, he lost his balance and fell, and the swan bowl flew out of his hands and smashed against the path.

And all mixed up with the sound of splintering glass and screaming cats, came the voice of his father.

"Adam!"

His father rarely shouted at him.

Adam got up shakily. His left knee was scratched and his elbows hurt, and all around him fragments of cut-glass lay scattered over the path. The lovely swan head, snapped from its slender neck, lay in the gravel. Adam felt awful. Adam felt terrible. He felt like a murderer. Tears began rolling down his cheeks.

"I didn't mean to break it," he wailed. "It was an accident."

His father looked at him grimly. "Of course it was an accident!" He was still shouting. "I saw the whole thing. You don't suppose I would think you'd broken it on purpose, do you? But what in heaven's name were you doing with it in the first place? If you needed a bowl to take into the garden there are plenty of plastic ones. You know very well the things in that cupboard are special! Why did you take it?"

Adam stared at the ground and went on crying. He didn't know what to say. He couldn't explain about the bird when his dad was so cross, and he certainly couldn't show it to him. And what was his mum going to say? The swan bowl was one of her favourite things.

"And another thing," his dad said in that

tight, unfamiliar voice, "I spotted this on the common on my way home," and he held out Adam's new school bag, forgotten among the ferns. "What's the matter with you?"

Just then his mother and Aunt Sarah came through the kitchen.

"I'll see you at the shop on Tuesday, Josie," said Aunt Sarah. "We can have lunch." She smiled at Adam's dad. "Hello, Robert, you're home early."

Then she saw the broken glass and Adam's tear-streaked face.

"Oh, dear!" she said. "Oh, what a shame."

His mother stared at the shattered remains of the bowl.

"Oh, no!" she said. "Not the swan bowl. Oh, Adam, what happened?"

Adam knew how upset she must be and he wept even more.

Aunt Sarah gave a tactful cough.

"Well, I'll be off, then," she announced brightly. She patted Adam on the head. "You're in big trouble now, young man."

Chapter Five

Mum bathed Adam's knee with iodine and brought him a drink. She looked weepy.

His dad was still cross.

"He left his bag out in the field as well. I found it when I walked across the common, just dumped on the grass. What's the matter with you, Adam?"

Mum put an arm round his shoulders. Adam squirmed. It didn't help. She should have been cross. She should have been furious. He would have been. He wished she would yell and shout, like other people's mums, instead of asking him wriggly questions.

"This isn't like you, Adam," she said.

"There's something wrong, isn't there? Did you have a rotten time at school today?"

Adam shook his head. He didn't feel like talking.

"So what exactly were you doing with that bowl?" asked his dad.

Adam felt the tears starting up again.

"I'll buy you another one just like it," he said miserably.

But his mother smiled sadly.

"I'm afraid that would be a bit difficult, love. It belonged to your great-grandmother, remember? It was very old..."

"I'd still like to know why you took it," his father persisted.

Adam swallowed hard.

This was not how he had wanted it to be. He had wanted to take them to see the bird. He had wanted to show it off. He had wanted to share his secret with them proudly, not like this. Now it was all spoilt.

But what else could he say? He took a deep breath.

"I found this bird you see," he began unimpressively. "I was taking it some water."

"In my granny's swan bowl?" said his mother sharply.

This was the hard bit.

"Well, it isn't an ordinary bird, you see. It's all silver and it's got bits of glass and crystals and things ... they could be real diamonds!" He heard himself and he sounded silly, but he went on desperately. "It's got real toes, like people's toes, only they're silver, and it's got sort of star things all over its back and it's got funny huge eyes, not like a bird's eyes at all, and its crest is all jewelly..."

His voice tailed off. He had said all the wrong things again – he could tell from the expressions on their faces. Even his dad was looking slightly amused, and his mother was actually smiling.

"Well, I do have to say – that's the prettiest excuse for scattiness I've ever heard," she said. "Will you draw us a picture of it..."

"It's a good story, Adam," added his father

drily, "but it's no excuse."

They didn't believe him. Well, of course they didn't – how could they?

"Look," he said. "It is real. It's a real bird. I can show it to you if you like."

His parents looked at each other in that secret way which always made him feel uncomfortable.

Then his mum said slowly, as if she had learnt the words by heart: "Adam, I think things as marvellous as your bird ought to be private, don't you?" And she gave him a hug. "Look," she went on, "I'm really upset about that bowl: I won't pretend I'm not, but I can see that you are, too. I know you're sorry, and I know that you won't do such a stupid thing again, so let's not talk about it any more, shall we? Early supper for you tonight because some people from your dad's office are coming over."

Adam stared at her.

"Mum!" he shouted. "It is real. I can show you. Right now."

But his mum only smiled understandingly and said: "Of course it is, love. Now, what do you want with your omelette – baked beans or chips?"

"And next time I find your satchel in a field, you can take your stuff to school in a supermarket bag," said his dad.

So that was that.

Adam sighed. Grown-ups always thought they knew everything; well, this time they were wrong.

He made one last attempt when his mum came up later to kiss him goodnight.

"It is real, Mum," he told her. "I could still show it to you." Downstairs he could hear someone laughing.

"In the morning, love," she whispered.

He gave up. What was the point?

He took out his torch and pulled out the Batman comic he'd hidden behind the chest of drawers. He started to read it but soon lost interest. Too many things had happened today and his eyes were still stinging from all that crying. He listened to the voices downstairs as he snuggled under the bedclothes.

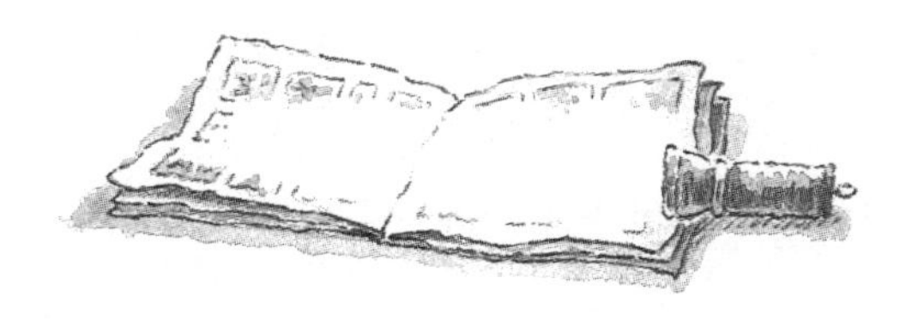

Chapter Six

In the middle of the night, Adam woke up. He looked at the luminous hands on his watch. Three o'clock. Not even night but morning.

A word kept running round inside his head – water. Water? Why "water"? He didn't feel thirsty.

Puzzled and still half asleep, he padded across to the bathroom and drank a few mouthfuls, just to make sure.

But when he slid back under his duvet, the word was still there. Water. Water. This time he made himself wake up properly. Something was wrong; he knew something was wrong.

Something to do with the bird...

Water. Of course. How could he have been so stupid?

He got out of bed. He put on his slippers and pulled a jumper over his head. Floorboards creaked as he crept downstairs but by that time the word was shouting itself: Water! Water! Water!

"All right, all right," he whispered.

He took a bowl – one of his mum's plastic mixing bowls – and filled it with water. Then he unbolted the back door and stepped out into the moonlit garden.

From somewhere in the bushes a cat howled – no longer a soft, furry pet but a tiger hunting in a forest. Moonlight drew funny, black shadows round things, changing their shapes. Even the dustbin wore a witch's hat.

Adam's voice was a little wobbly.

"I'm coming, bird."

He stepped warily across the garden, past the compost heap and around the brambles and nettles. He opened the summer-house door. Hesitantly, he looked inside, and there, on the shelf, was the bird, all moon-jewelled, ruffling its glassy feathers with its glittering beak.

Holding his breath, Adam carefully lowered the bowl. The water see-sawed, splashing his hands.

The bird turned its head slowly from side to side, as if it were checking on Adam's offering. Then it opened its beak, and a thin, silver vein, like a coiled-up drinking straw, unrolled from somewhere within its throat.

Inside Adam's head, words spoke themselves: this world is a good place.

Well, yes, thought Adam; suppose it's OK.

And the shadow of the water moved down and down until the bowl was quite empty, and Adam's own tummy felt comfortably full, as if he had just eaten the most delicious of suppers, and he felt delightfully drowsy, as if he had just had a bubble bath, and had towelled himself dry, and was ready to curl up in his bed.

Dreamily, sleepily, he held out his hand.

Come here, bird, he thought.

And with a tinkling and a shimmering of feathers, the bird flew down to perch on his oustretched palm, turning and nuzzling against his chest in the way Mopsie did when she was feeling affectionate. Adam was amazed. Birds aren't like cats, he thought; they don't go in for that sort of thing. But then, his bird was different.

He stood for a long, long time, stroking its cold, spiky body. At last, reluctantly, he lowered it gently on to the shelf.

"See you tomorrow," he whispered, and he picked up the bowl, pushed back the stone and ran across the garden to the house.

In the morning, when his mum came in to wake him for school, everything looked grey and ordinary. Downstairs, cornflakes nestled in a pool of milk, and a brown egg sat in the chicken egg-cup just like it always did. And there was his satchel, smelling of school, and there was the dinner-money next to his plate. School dinners – yuk! Who wanted to think about school dinners?

"You look tired, Adam," his mum said. "You still worrying about that bowl?"

"A bit." Adam lied.

"Well, don't. What's done's done and worrying won't bring it back."

"I don't think I feel very well," Adam said hopefully, passing his hand over his forehead. "I've got a headache and a sore throat." The prospect of a whole lovely day spent at home spread out before him.

His mother felt his head. She made him open his mouth. She peered down his throat.

"I don't think there's much wrong with you, young man," she said at last.

Adam sighed: she was getting so hard to fool.

"If it does get any worse," she said briskly, "tell Miss Thomas, love, won't you? The secretary knows where to find me." She brought him his coat and kissed him goodbye.

"Off you go, now, or you'll be late. Your dad's got the car today or I'd give you a lift.

Don't leave your bag on the common again!" she called after him.

On the way out, he walked round to the summer-house and peered through its grimy windows. The bird was still there; he could see it, shimmering among the cobwebs. He longed to take it out and stroke it, to feel it nuzzling against his chest again, but there simply wasn't time.

All the way to school he kept thinking about it.

He wished he'd been able to tell his parents. He badly needed their help. He needed someone's help. It was all very well pretending that the bird was his special pet, but that wasn't enough. He needed to know more about it. What was it? What did it live on? If it died because he was too mean to share it or to ask the right questions, it would be his fault, wouldn't it?

He decided to make a start on finding out.

He would begin by borrowing some books about birds from the school library.

Chapter Seven

"Quake, Quake, Shivery-Shake," someone called as Adam walked across the playground, but today he hardly noticed. He was too busy thinking.

What was he going to do about his bird? Even if he did persuade it to eat something (nuts? worms?) he couldn't go on keeping it inside the summer-house – a bird couldn't fly in such a small space. And there was still that other question: did it belong to anyone? Had it come from a zoo? Had it flown in from some faraway place?

The bell rang, and he joined the rest of his class. Drearily, the pattern of the day began to unfold. Assembly. Register. History – who cared? The hands of the big clock on the wall seemed to move hardly at all. Playtime, and no one to play with, but today he was glad, because he could spend the time in the library, browsing through the big natural history encyclopaedia. But there was nothing remotely like his bird in any of them.

And after playtime, a video about Australia. Adam grinned as he dutifully drew his picture of a wallaby. Wallabies funny? Wallabies strange? Miss Thomas should take a look inside his summer-house.

Dinnertime came, with its warm, stifling smell of gravy. Adam sighed. It was liver and he wasn't hungry and he would never get through the afternoon.

But then something unusual happened. Miss Thomas appeared with someone else. A new teacher. A student, she explained, and they were all to behave very nicely.

Adam looked at the student. Her hair was dark and curly, and her face was jolly, but she acted a bit scared. She was carrying a small tape recorder, which she set up on Miss Thomas's desk. Suddenly Adam was as curious as everyone else.

Miss Thomas left with a pile of exercise books.

The student sat down in Miss Thomas's chair. She smiled at them nervously and gave a little cough.

"I've brought some music for you," she said. Her voice was quite loud. "I chose it specially and I hope you'll like it."

"Got any Michael Jackson tapes, Miss?"

They giggled.

"Or Madonna?"

"Oh yuk! Not Madonna."

The class was getting noisy.

Suddenly the room was filled with music. The music was much louder than the giggles. It wasn't the sort of stuff they usually had at school – it had drums and electric guitars.

Some of the girls began fooling about.

"Ooh, give us more, Miss," pleaded Sharon.

But instead, the student began to talk. She talked about pop music and jazz, and as she talked, her voice grew softer, so they really had to listen. They liked the way she told them things, not bossy but as if they were her friends. Most people settled down to listen.

She put on another tape.

"This music comes from the Andes," she said.

A girl teased: "Andy-Pandy?" but the others said: "S-s-s-h!"

It was funny, breathy music and Adam liked it.

The student began talking above the tape.

"Close your eyes," she said. "That way you can listen better. See what the music makes you think of. Afterwards, I'd like each of you to make a picture."

They giggled again – it did sound a bit daft.

"Ssh!" said the student, and this time, they did.

Adam put his hands over his face and let the music wash over him like a big wave. He tried to see pictures inside his head. He tried very hard, but nothing came, so he stopped trying. You can't, he thought, see things just because someone tells you to, so he let his thoughts drift back to where they wanted to go. The bird. His bird. He remembered its strange, twinkly neck and the little needles of glass which seemed to grow out of its tummy. He thought about its patterns of overlapping stars, and the way the wings extended in shining curves, and how it made all those little rainbows when the sun shone.

Someone was pushing past his desk. The

music had stopped, and people were squabbling over paint-pots, and pulling stuff out of a large cardboard box.

"Wake up, or you won't have time to do your picture," the student teased.

So Adam got up and joined the others.

The box was full of papers. There was tissue paper in soft colours, and gift wrapping paper. There were pages torn from magazines, bronze and blue sweet papers, and even flattened milk bottle tops in silver and gold. Adam liked making pictures, and he knew exactly how this one was going to be – the details of it were so clear in his mind that it almost felt like cheating.

He returned to his seat with a handful of stuff, regretting that the best things had already gone. He sorted it out and began to work. He worked slowly and with great concentration, because he wanted to make the bird as real as possible. It was an excuse to show it off, secretly, without giving anything away.

He was still working long after the others had finished. People strolled over to watch.

"Smashing, what is it?" somebody asked.

"It's a Quaker quaking."

"It's a butterfly."

There were shouts of protest.

"With legs like that? Don't be stupid!"

"It's a bird."

"It's an angel."

"It's a fairy! It's the Shivery-Shake fairy! Look, Miss, Adam's done the Shivery-Shake fairy," and they collapsed into giggles.

Seeing Adam's pink cheeks, the student hurried over.

"But it's lovely!" she said. "It's smashing! And does it really matter what it is? You can't always give names to things, you know. I'm going to put this one up on the wall, if I may."

She looked questioningly at Adam, but he nodded yes. You never said no to a teacher.

She picked it up carefully, and the little group scattered as she went from desk to desk, looking at everyone's work. But Adam went on sitting there, his cheeks still burning. It was always the same, he thought: no matter how hard he tried, it always came out wrong. He felt as if he had just put his bird into a cage and shown it around for them all to laugh at.

Quickly, he sorted out his things, hiding his face behind his bag. The student, pinning up pictures, looked across at him and grinned.

"I'm sorry but I can't remember your name."

"Adam."

"Well, good work, then, Adam. I like that picture of yours."

The bell sounded the end of the afternoon. At last he could escape. The others were milling round the student so Adam slipped out quietly. In the cloakroom, he grabbed his coat, thankful that there were still not too many kids around, and ran out into the playground.

Behind him, someone called out: "Hey! I liked that picture you did."

And Adam winced.

Chapter Eight

Adam glanced round slyly to see who was teasing him this time. It was Gary.

He began to walk faster, but Gary ran after him.

"Where you going so fast?"

"Home," said Adam. "Where d'you think?"

"Hey, listen. That picture you did."

Shut up, shut up, thought Adam. He sighed. "What about it?"

"Well, it was like something from that science fiction film. That one about those giant insects – you know. You into science fiction?"

Did Batman count? "Well, sort of."

"Great! I mean, not many people are. My brother's got masses. Most people think it's stupid."

Was it stupid? Adam had never thought about it. He tried to say something more about it, but Gary just went on talking.

"Was it a bird? I mean, it looked a bit like a bird, except for those eyes ... and those feet..." He giggled. "You gave it toes, you dope! Birds don't have toes."

"Some of them do," said Adam quickly.

"Listen," said Gary. "I'm telling you: birds don't have toes. My dad keeps racing pigeons and I know. Bet you've never seen a racing pigeon?"

"No, I haven't."

"They're really something! I mean, they look just like ordinary pigeons but you can fly them for hundreds of miles and they always come back. Our lot are the fastest. They're champs. People put bets on them, like racehorses." He hesitated. "Want to see?"

Did he really mean it?

"Thanks," said Adam shyly. "That'd be great."

He looked sideways at Gary. Gary's satchel had patches and badges. Gary was in the football team. His dad was a long-distance lorry driver, and his mum was one of the school dinner-ladies. Gary was tough. No one could make a fool out of him.

Right now, Adam needed someone sensible.

He needed him badly.

All that stuff about science fiction had bothered him. Those pictures in the encyclopaedia – none of them looked like his

bird. He thought about it now. He thought about its rainbow-glitter feathers and its overlapping stars. He thought about its strange, transparent skin, and the silver toes, just like fingers, which had curled so lovingly round his hand.

There just weren't any birds like that. Not in England. Not in Africa. Not even in Australia.

Not anywhere on earth.

"What a lovely pretend," his mum had said. Well, supposing that was true? If he showed it to her, she might even pretend to see it, just to please him. How could he trust her? How could he be sure?

He could trust Gary.

"Want to come back and muck around at my place?" Adam asked the question casually, as if the answer didn't really matter.

He had to know if his bird was real. Because if it were real – and he formed the words slowly inside his head because the idea they made was so scary – if it were real, it couldn't possibly belong to the world he knew about.

"You got a big garden up there?"

Adam nodded.

Gary considered.

"OK," he said. "I'll have to leave a note for my mum, though. How long can I stay?"

"Long as you like." Adam felt pleased. He knew exactly what to do: he'd just worked it out.

He would say nothing about the bird – that bit would be easy. They'd fool around for a while, kick a ball about, or swing. Gary would get bored and want to do something else; then Adam would take him to the summer-house. Then if he saw the bird and Gary didn't, Adam would know. But if they both saw it.

Well, Gary was used to handling birds; he wouldn't do anything stupid. It would mean sharing his secret, but he'd have to share it with someone, because if it was true, then it was too big to hold all by himself.

Gary's house was in a small, quiet street. Over its front door there was a garland of stone flowers which someone had picked out in bright colours. In the front garden, greasy bits of motor-bike lay between sunflowers, geraniums and pots of ripening tomatoes.

"My brother's," jeered Gary. "He'll get it to work one day, I don't think..."

He scribbled a note and propped it against the front room window. Somewhere above their heads, a pigeon cooed.

Adam wondered if it were one of the racers, and how you got pigeons to race anyway, and for a while, his curiosity about these things made him forget about his other problems.

"That one of yours?"

"Yeah."

"How d'you teach them?"

"Teach them what?"

"How to race?"

Gary considered the question.

"Tell you if you tell me something."

"What?"

"You really quake?"

Adam lost his patience.

"Don't be stupid!"

"What you do then?"

"Nothing much. I mean, nothing ... I mean, it's like church only nobody talks much."

"People don't talk in church anyway, dope. That all? That all you do? Thought you did something wild." He sounded disappointed.

"Pigeons," said Adam. "Come on. Tell me."

And so absorbed were they in their conversation that the long walk over to Adam's house seemed no distance at all. And Adam found himself wondering vaguely why it was suddenly so easy to talk to someone. Then, secretly, he laughed at himself.

He wasn't talking at all.

He was listening.

Chapter Nine

Adam's mum came out of the kitchen. He willed her to say the right things – not to look too pleased, not to fuss and flap over Gary.

But all she said was: "Hello, love – I've only just this minute got in. You didn't tell me you were bringing a friend home for tea or I'd have bought something."

"That's all right," said Gary. "I don't eat much at this time anyway – I have my supper later when my dad gets back. I just came over to play."

"Would either of you be interested in some crisps?"

"You bet!" said Gary. "What flavour?"

A few minutes later, Adam, licking the salt from his lips, ran across the garden with Gary. For a moment, he had lost all interest in the reality of the bird.

They pottered around, kicking a ball, snapping off the brittle stems of cow parsley on the common, and climbing about in the big elm on the other side of the fence. For a while, Adam didn't care whether the bird was real or not. This was a lot of fun.

And Gary didn't get bored.

Adam had almost forgotten why he'd asked him back in the first place.

"Come and see our rotten old summer-house," he said at last. "It's all falling to bits."

Gary snorted. "Sounds great."

They walked round the side, to the neglected bit of the garden. They struggled through the blackberry bushes and the old raspberry canes, and there was the frail, rotting summer-house under its dark tangle of vine.

"Why d'you call it a summer-house? Looks more like a winter-house to me."

"Dunno."

"What d'you keep in there?"

Adam shrugged.

"Junk, mostly."

He moved the stone and the door sagged open.

At first nothing happened.

Then, like a streak of light, the bird flew out. It flew on to Adam's shoulder and nuzzled its head against his neck.

Adam looked quickly at Gary.

Gary stood, frozen, his arms limp as a puppet's. His eyes were huge and his mouth was wide open, but, for the first time, he seemed to have nothing at all to say.

Then Adam knew.

They couldn't both be pretending.

"What is it?" said Gary at last. His voice came out small and croaky.

"A bird."

"Yours?"

"Sort of."

Gary moved. He walked very slowly round, looking all the time at the bird. Then he scratched his head.

"See what you mean about the toes."

Adam grinned.

"Can I touch it?"

"Suppose so," Adam said reluctantly. "But please be careful."

Timidly, Gary put out one finger and touched the bird's head. When nothing extraordinary happened, he grew a bit bolder, lingering over the shining crest, and wondrously tracing the star patterns on its wings.

"It was real, then," he said at last.

"Yes."

Gary thought about it.

"That picture you did," he said slowly. "Hey! You cheated."

"I know. Listen. Don't tell anybody, will you?"

"That you cheated?"

"Don't be silly. I mean, about the bird."

"Don't you want to show it off? If it was mine I'd be telling everyone."

"Well, it's not yours."

"All right, all right." Gary hesitated. Then he asked shyly: "Would it – he – come to me, d'you think?"

And straight away – almost as if it had understood – the bird, in a flurry of sparkles, flew on to Gary's shoulder. Gary ducked in terror, then recovered.

"Oh, bird," he whispered. "You're a beauty."

Adam felt a sudden pang of jealousy. It was his bird, wasn't it? Would it go to just anybody then?

Immediately, as if to reassure him, the bird flew back and nuzzled against his neck. Adam stroked it gratefully. It had understood.

Adam understood something too – the word inside his head. He glared fiercely at Gary.

"Water," he said.

Gary looked baffled.

"Water," Adam insisted.

"OK, OK, don't be bossy – can't you get your own water?" Gary ran back to the kitchen and returned with a full tumbler.

"Not enough," said Adam. "Go back. Find the white plastic bowl. Fill it."

Gary was irritated.

"Fetch it yourself!" he said. "Fill it yourself!"

"Not for me," said Adam.

"Oh."

Gary came back more slowly, hugging the plastic bowl against his chest. He lowered it cautiously on to the shelf. The bird flew in, and began to drink.

Gary jumped back in alarm.

"How does he do that?"

"Don't know."

"Don't know much, do you?"

"No I don't..."

"So where does he come from? Where did you get him?"

So Adam told him the whole story.

When he had finished, Gary said: "Does your mum know?"

Adam shook his head.

"Shouldn't you ... I mean, shouldn't you tell her? I mean, she'll find out anyway, won't she?"

"Why should she?" said Adam. "She never comes anywhere near this place. Neither of them do. Anyway, I tried to tell her yesterday but she wouldn't listen so I gave up on it."

"Well try again. Show her. How about your dad?"

"Oh my dad's a dead loss."

"Well you ought to tell someone," said Gary slowly. "I mean, people ought to know... I'd like to show it to my dad." He suddenly thought of something. "It is real, isn't it? I mean, you're not having me on, are you? I mean, it isn't some kind of a trick, is it? Magic Show stuff? Listen, if you're having me on..."

"It's real all right."

"Well can I tell my dad?"

"Not if I don't tell my mum."

There was a moment of silence.

Then Gary said, "All right. I suppose that's fair."

"I mean, I want to keep it a secret – at least for now."

"OK. You're on. Hey, listen – thanks for letting me in on it. I won't say a word – honest cross my heart. Tell me something, though – what's it live on? I mean, it can't just have water and nothing else. Has it eaten anything?"

"No."

"Well we'd better try it on things. First thing we need to know is whether it's carnivorous or a seed eater. We need to catch some insects – flies and things. You got any poppies? Or sunflower seeds? Listen, we got plenty of birdseed at my place. Top quality stuff... I could bring you in a whole bagful tomorrow."

Chapter Ten

Fly-catching wasn't as easy as the boys had supposed, and soon it turned into a silly game which sent them falling about in the grass. Adam's mum, baffled, watched from the kitchen window.

"Whatever are you two up to?" she called.

"Catching flies!" shouted Adam.

"Oh, yes."

Then Gary had an idea.

"Ants," he said. "And small spiders. They're easier. Ladybirds if there are any left."

"Oh not ladybirds," protested Adam. "I like ladybirds."

There were no more ants but Gary found things – a couple of spiders, a woodlouse, and a fly caught in a web. Adam found nothing.

Gary scraped off his kill on a flat stone.

Adam shivered.

"Your mum got tweezers?"

"Think so." Grateful to be doing something useful, Adam ran up to the bathroom.

"Thanks," said Gary. "Now we can put all the corpses on a saucer."

"Yuk," said Adam.

"You're too soft," said Gary. "It's nature – there's nothing wrong with nature. Things eat things."

They carried the squashy mess back to the summer-house. The bird showed no interest.

"Oh, well," said Gary, "seed-eater. Just as well, really – he wouldn't get much with you around."

They wandered on to the common in search of poppy-heads and fennel. In twilight it was difficult to spot things, but Gary was good at it – he knew just where to look.

They found a big leaf and spread the seeds out on it. Like that, they looked delicious. They looked so good that they could almost have eaten them themselves, but the bird wasn't interested.

"I give up," said Gary. "Maybe fruit."

Adam was stroking the bird's head.

"Not fruit either," he said dreamily.

"How do you know, Big-head? Some birds eat fruit."

"Not your fruit. Not your insects. Not your seeds," said Adam. "It cannot digest your life-forms."

Gary stared at him open-mouthed.

"You flipped?" he asked.

Adam ignored him.

"It can feed on itself now," he said. "You see, the time of the Change has come."

"What change? What you talking about?"

"Water is all that it needs now."

"What on earth are you going on about?"

Adam was suddenly confused.

"I – I don't know," he said. "Forget it."

His mum called from the kitchen steps.

"Gary, I don't want to rush you but it's nearly seven."

"Crikey!" said Gary. "I'd better get back."

Adam walked part of the way with him.

Gary was quiet. Something was bothering him.

"You were talking all funny back there," he said at last.

"Oh I do that sometimes," said Adam quickly. He was feeling embarrassed. Why had he said all those stupid things? He

couldn't remember half of them himself, and he didn't understand any of them.

But he had to invent some kind of explanation, or Gary would think he was cuckoo.

"I make things up to catch people out," he announced boldly. "Caught you, didn't I?"

Gary frowned.

"D'you mean the bird?"

"Oh, no. Not that. Not the bird. Honest."

"You wouldn't."

"No. I told you. Honest."

"Can I come back tomorrow, then?"

"If you like," said Adam, concealing his own pleasure at being asked.

"I won't tell anyone. You can trust me. What a secret – wow! Listen. I'll bring some proper birdseed tomorrow, like I said. The best – we've got plenty at home."

Chapter Eleven

They didn't say much to each other at school the next morning, but once, Gary held up a brown paper bag, and winked at Adam.

At playtime, though, kicking a ball around with friends, Gary spotted Adam sitting alone on the bench.

"Want to be goalie?" he shouted.

The other boys groaned.

"Not him. Not the Shivery-Shake!"

"You off your rocker, Gary?"

"Not the Quake, Quake, Quaker."

Gary grabbed one of them by the belt.

"What d'you know about Quakers, Fat-Face?"

"Nothing."

"Then shut it! This bloke's a friend of mine."

"Since when?"

"Mind your own business."

Adam kept on missing the ball.

"Told you," someone sneered.

Then by accident his foot caught it and sent it sailing across the playground.

"Cor!" they shouted.

"Not bad," said Gary. "You just need practice."

"Why," he asked Adam on the way home, "d'you let people say those things?"

"What things?"

"Quake, Quake, Shivery-Shake. Anyone said that to me, I'd smash them."

Adam took a deep breath.

"Quakers aren't supposed to."

"Supposed to what?"

"Hit people."

"Oh..." Gary thought about it. "What you do if people hit you first?"

"Dunno, really." Adam grinned nervously. "Run."

As they walked across Adam's garden, Gary suddenly punched him in the back.

"Ow!" said Adam. "What's that for?"

"Wanted to find out."

"Find out what?"

"What you'd do."

"That's not fair," said Adam.

"I know," said Gary. "So go on. Hit me! Hit me! I deserve it."

"Don't want to."

"Punch me! Go on, punch me back..."

Adam clenched his fists until they hurt.

"I won't," he said. "I won't."

"Oh forget it," said Gary. "Listen, I'm sorry." He put an arm around Adam's shoulders. "Listen – you're OK."

They walked round to the summer-house with the bag of seeds. Adam was feeling bothered – annoyed with Gary and cross with himself.

Inside the summer-house, nothing moved.

"Come on, bird," coaxed Gary, but no shimmer of light fluttered out to greet them.

Suddenly Adam was scared.

"You look," he whispered to Gary. "Go on."

And Gary stepped reluctantly inside.

The bird was still perched on the shelf, but it didn't seem to have noticed him. It looked smaller now, and its body sagged as if it were much too heavy for its feet, and its tail drooped like a piece of tarnished tinsel.

Gary looked back at Adam.

"It's gone all funny."

Adam pushed past him. They stood in silence.

"We could put it in a box," said Gary at last, "and take it to the vet."

But Adam put out a finger and touched the bird's head. It was quite cold.

"It's too late," he said. "It's dead."

"You can't be sure," said Gary hopefully. "It could be sleeping."

"It's dead," said Adam in a small, hard voice. "I know it is."

Adam's mum called from the kitchen.

"Come on, boys! I've made you some pancakes."

They walked out of the summer-house. Adam fastened the door, and kicked back the stone. Not knowing what else to do, the two of them walked in silence to the house.

The kitchen was full of the warm, sweet smell of cooking, and on the table lay a plate piled high with pancakes. Adam's mum filled two glasses with lemonade.

"I'm prepared for you today, Gary," she joked.

The boys sat down like a couple of robots.

The thought of food made Adam feel sick, but he didn't want to hurt his mother's feelings. He picked up a pancake, sprinkled it with sugar and lemon juice and bit into it, but it tasted of nothing. He filled up his mouth with it, swallowing it back quickly. Tears pricked his eyes. He blinked and forced them back. An uncomfortable silence filled the room, and his mother's attempts to break it only made things worse.

"You're a glum pair of chaps – what's wrong? Don't you like pancakes, Gary?"

"They're great," muttered Gary, fiddling with his fork.

"Well for goodness' sake eat them before they get cold. I'll leave the two of you to get on with it."

After she had left, they began sniping at each other.

"It was your fault ... you should have told her."

"Well I didn't!"

"Perhaps it's not really..."

"It's dead all right. You saw it. You blind?"

"Shall we go and...?"

"No."

Silence.

"Well what are you going to do?" Gary

corrected himself. "What are we going to do?"

"What do you think? What you do with dead things."

"What?"

"Bury them, stupid."

"We ought to show it to someone first."

"What's the point?"

Silence.

Finally Gary stood up.

"I'm going home," he said.

But Adam didn't even look up.

"I'm sorry," said Gary awkwardly. "I'm really sorry. It was a smashing pet. It was a beauty." He was nearly crying. "I'll help you bury it if you like."

But Adam still said nothing.

"So long, then."

Chapter Twelve

Adam went on sitting at the table, not moving.

Gary was right, he thought bitterly – it was all his fault. He should have told someone. Someone else, not Gary. A grown-up: somebody who would have known what to do. He should have made his mother listen. He should have made her come out and look. He should have shown the bird to his dad. He could have told Miss Thomas. He could have tried the Animal Shelter people. He could have rung the zoo. Now it was too late. The bird was dead.

When his mum came back and saw him still sitting there, she frowned and looked worried.

"Gary left?"

He nodded miserably.

She put an arm around him.

"You two had a quarrel? Don't worry – it isn't the end of the world. You'll make it up tomorrow – you'll see. I'm sorry about the pancakcs though."

She irritated him.

Adam muttered something and wandered out into the garden. For a while he messed about, doing nothing, carefully avoiding that dark corner behind the compost heap. Pulling off a rose-head, he crushed it between his fingers, wishing bitterly that Gary had stayed – he needed someone to punch.

At last he shuffled round the corner to the summer-house. He had to. Perhaps it wasn't true. Perhaps the bird had just been sleeping after all.

He pushed away the stone and opened the door.

The bird lay glimmering on the shelf. In the half-light of evening it looked even smaller. Its head and feet had completely vanished inside itself, and its ragged, pathetic tail wrapped its body in silvery tissue.

It frightened him but he made himself touch it. Its feathers felt cold and slightly sticky. His fingers were shaking but he curled them round the bird until he was holding it gently between his two hands. It was like holding an egg made of spun sugar.

"Tomorrow," he reminded himself grimly, "I will have to bury it."

He placed the fragile cocoon back on the shelf.

"Goodbye, bird," he whispered.

He struggled through the bushes, not caring if they scratched him.

And then, holding on to the fence, he let the tears come out, and he cried and cried until everything melted in water.

Somebody touched him.

"What's wrong, old chap?"

Adam looked up in a panic. He hadn't heard his dad coming through the gate.

He sniffled and choked.

"Oh, nothing much."

"Must be something," said Dad as they walked back to the house. "People don't cry like that over nothing at all."

Mum spotted his weepy face.

"Oh you mustn't get so upset, love. Quarrels are soon mended. He and Gary had a quarrel this afternoon," she explained.

Adam let them believe it. It was the simplest thing to do.

"Saw an ad. in the paper for a second-hand bike," said his father casually. "Would suit eight to ten year old, it said. We might go along and take a look at it this week-end."

Adam put on a smile to please him.

"That's better," said Mum. "Now blow your nose and come and have some supper."

But supper was as difficult to eat as the pancakes had been.

At last he gave up.

"Not really hungry."

"It'll all seem better after a good night's sleep," said Mum. "You'll see. Off you go."

In bed he lay stiffly, staring up at the ceiling. He had lost his bird. He had lost his friend. He had lost everything.

On the bookshelf the cover of *The Observer Book of Birds* seemed to taunt him, and he snatched it and hurled it against the wall so that its cover twisted and its pages crumpled.

His mum came to see what the noise was about. When she saw the book all mangled and torn, she was furious.

"You may be miserable," she said, "but that's no way to treat a book," and she took it away.

Adam didn't care. He was glad the book was wrecked: it hadn't helped, had it? And he was glad that his mum was angry. He wanted people to be angry with him. He wanted people to hate him. He hated himself.

With stinging eyes, he stared into the growing darkness. Somewhere in the town, he heard a clock strike eleven. He heard his parents going to bed. He heard their voices murmuring away in the darkness, and wondered what they were talking about. Him, he supposed. About what a dead loss he was. About how he couldn't ever keep a friend...

At last, he slept.

Chapter Thirteen

Adam woke up with a headache, but he didn't tell his mum.

"Feeling better, love?"

Feeling awful, he nodded.

He could have tried for a day off school. This time, he didn't need to put on much of an act: he might even have got away with it. But if he stayed home, there would be nothing to do but think, and sooner or later he would have to go out there. He couldn't just leave it. He'd have to...

No. Not yet.

School was ordinary, but right now Adam needed things to be ordinary.

And teachers were bossy, but right now, Adam wouldn't have minded someone telling him what to do.

He knew what to do, but he could do it afterwards. Later. When he came home. And he had to do it by himself. Gary was out of it now. It was Adam's responsibility. It had been Adam's bird. The "had been" made him feel sick.

His mum gave him a lift to school.

"Cheer up, love," she said when she kissed him goodbye. "You'll make it up."

He wandered dismally into the playground.

One or two people spotted him.

"Hi, Adam."

"Hi."

He looked for Gary, but he wasn't around. Adam was glad; he couldn't have known what to say to him anyway...

For half the morning, he worked at maths. Circles and triangles. Cubes and rectangles. So what? Those problems were easy. You got them right and you got a tick. You got them wrong, so you got them wrong. Nothing got hurt.

Not like people.

Not like animals.

Not like birds...

Just before the dinner bell, Gary turned up.

When Miss Thomas read the note he'd given her, she put a hand on his shoulder and whispered something. The other kids noticed. They glanced at Gary as he sat down. Even Adam was curious.

When the dinner bell rang, Gary was surrounded.

"Where you been?"

"What happened to you?"

But Adam sat at another table, and afterwards, in the playground, he avoided Gary, slinking round by the back fence to be by himself.

They found him, watching the seagulls in the field.

"Hey, you!"

"Hey, Shivery-Shake, we're setting up a team."

"Hey, Shivery-Shake, want to be goalie?"

What did Adam have to lose? Nothing, he thought. Nothing now. He shrugged.

"OK."

He walked back with them.

"Gary, you in?"

"No thanks."

"We've got the Shivery-Shake."

Gary looked annoyed.

"Hey, listen! He has got a name."

"OK, OK."

"Adam! Madam!"

"Adam! Get it!"

"Come on, Adam!"

Adam pranced about like a monkey, concentrating on nothing but the game, but when the ball came flying at him, it reminded him of that stupid egg-thing his bird had turned into, or Gary's thick head, and he kicked out at it with such ferocity that his foot hurt.

"Save!"

"Gotcher!"

"Get it, Adam! Go on! Kill him!"

"We are the champions!"

When the bell rang, and they'd all calmed down, Gary came over. He still looked a bit funny.

"You got talent," he said.

Adam said nothing. Gary hung about.

"You done it?" he whispered.

"Done what?"

"You know..."

"Not yet."

"I'll still help."

But Adam didn't want to talk about it.

"Why were you so late?" he asked quickly.

Gary stared at the ground.

"Oh that," he said reluctantly. "It was my dad. Lorry jack-knifed. On the motorway."

Adam was shocked. He didn't know what jack-knifing was but it sounded awful.

"Is he...?" Not more hurting, he prayed. And, oh please, not more dying.

"Oh he's OK ... just, you know, all shook up. It was my mum, this morning... Flipped her lid when they told her. See you after school – OK?"

"Yes. OK."

At the end of the afternoon, they each hung around, waiting. Not speaking much, feeling uneasy with each other, they began to walk home.

"What's jack-knifing?" Adam asked finally.

"Oh that. It's when the load turns at right angles to the cabin."

Adam nodded, feeling stupid.

"There were a couple of near-misses before the police came and he was – well, scared, upset – I mean, wouldn't you be? They're keeping him in hospital till tomorrow. My mum's in there with him."

They came to the turn-off for Gary's street. Gary hesitated.

"Can I come back to your place?"

"Don't you want to go and see your dad?"

"I can see him tomorrow. He don't like fusses."

"Well... OK, then," said Adam reluctantly.

They walked on in silence. But what was a bird, thought Adam, even his star-bird, compared with a real person? Compared with someone's dad?

When he thought of something happening to his dad, he shivered.

Chapter Fourteen

The boys walked across the edge of the common.

People from the houses had been collecting junk for a bonfire, and on the scrubby patch in the middle, the pile was growing.

"Your lot having a bonfire?"

"The Meeting House does a big one," said Adam, "so we don't bother."

Gary was curious.

"That what you call your church?"

Adam nodded.

"What a funny name."

They opened the gate.

Adam wondered who was playing a radio –

it wasn't his mum's kind of music.

From around the corner, staggering under a sheaf of brambles, came a lad in torn jeans and grass-stained trainers.

Adam was startled.

"What are you doing in our garden?" he demanded.

The boy dropped the brambles and jeered at him: "What you think?"

Adam's mum came out of the kitchen. When she saw Gary, she looked pleased.

"Hello, you two! This is Steve. I've got him to clear away the old brambles for us – about time that mess was sorted out."

Adam began to shiver.

"But I've got ... things in that summer-house."

"Oh he hasn't cleared the summer-house..."

"I'm going to look." Adam's voice sounded choked.

Steve looked amused.

"I haven't touched a thing – honest!"

Gary ran after Adam.

Steve tapped one finger on his partly shaved head. "Barmy, kids." Adam's mum shrugged.

"Would you like a cup of tea?"

"Got any Pepsi? Hot work, this." The summer-house was no longer a secret. With its brambles and its veil of vine all torn away, it was just a dirty old shack, but the stone still lay against the door.

Adam pulled it away and stepped fearfully inside. He closed his eyes, then made himself open them. He looked. There lay the smooth, silvery egg-thing. Adam sighed with relief. He picked it up gently, cradling it in his hands.

"Is it OK?" whispered Gary.

Adam brought it out and showed it to him.

"What do we do?" Gary corrected himself. "What'll you do?"

"Nothing," said Adam. His voice came out strong and confident. "Wait till it's dark. Then take it back. To the place where it landed."

"Landed?" Gary chuckled. "What you mean, landed? It's not an aeroplane."

"It will be taken back."

"You gone all funny again."

"It is not dead."

"Sorry, Adam, but it looks dead to me."

"It's not dead," said Adam in a more ordinary voice. "It's all right." He sounded surprised, happy. "It's sort of sleeping. Like caterpillars, you know?"

"No I don't."

"Yes you do. They go to sleep inside those cocoon things and wake up as butterflies."

"So it's going to wake up as a butterfly?"

"Don't be stupid."

"But how d'you know all that stuff? OK, OK. So you know. But we can't put it back in there – not with that bloke around."

"We can take it into the house – I mean, it doesn't look like anything much now. We can keep it in my room."

They walked back. Behind them, the summer-house door swung on its rusty hinge.

"Can I ring my mum at the hospital?" asked Gary.

“At the hospital?” Adam’s mother looked alarmed. “Is she ill?”

"No, it's my dad – he had a bit of an accident."

"Aren't you going in to see him?"

"No. He's OK, really. It was just for a check-up. They're sending him home tomorrow."

Adam ran upstairs, his fingers curled protectively round the smooth oval in his anorak pocket. Inside his room, he took it out and laid it on a cushion. It was funny – he didn't feel sad any more.

"It's not dead," he reminded himself. "It's sort of ... changing."

He closed the door carefully and went downstairs. Steve was finishing up in the garden.

"He needed the work," Mum explained. "And we needed to get it done. When those stems are dry, they can go on the big bonfire. Talking of which, look what I've got."

She opened the oven and brought out a tray of chestnuts, split and sizzling.

"Not as good as doing them on a real fire

but the next best thing."

They ate them greedily, scorching their fingers. Adam suddenly remembered that conker – had it really been...?

He grinned. He could guess what Gary'd say to that: Magic conkers? You must be bonkers!

Gary was fooling about with the charred bits of chestnut skin, stacking them up in a wobbly pile.

"I told my mum I was staying on for a bit – that OK?"

"That's fine. I'll run you home later."

Steve came for his money and left. The garden was theirs.

They fooled around, teasing next door's kitten, throwing chestnut skins at each other, listening to the odd firework popping, and watching the sky mellow into dusk.

My dad's late home tonight, Adam suddenly thought, with a new little curl of fear in the pit of his stomach.

Then he heard the car door slam, and his

parents talking. It was all right. He was OK.

"Why didn't you want to go and see your dad?" he asked Gary awkwardly.

Gary shrugged.

"Wasn't worth it, was it?"

Adam was shocked.

"If my dad'd had an accident like that jack-knifing thing ... well ... I'd be ... you know."

"D'you think I'm not?" said Gary fiercely.

"Well, I..."

Gary punched him in the chest. It wasn't a big punch but it knocked Adam breathless.

"Go on, I hit you for nothing. Go on, Shivery-Shake, hit me back! Hit me back!"

"I don't want to..." said Adam, bewildered.

"Listen. I don't know what your dad does, but mine's on the road for days at a stretch. And things happen. And if we worried at things the way you lot worry at things we'd be in a loony bin by now... Listen. I don't want to talk about it. OK?"

"OK," said Adam. "OK."

“It’s nearly time,” said Adam.

“You telling me to shove off?”

“The bird.”

“Oh...”

“I’ll go back and get it. You wait.”

“Fetch my coat, then. I’m cold.”

“OK.”

His parents were drinking coffee in the sitting room.

“’Lo, Dad.”

“That was brief,” said his dad.

“His friend’s still here,” his mum explained.

“We’re going out,” Adam announced. The precious egg lay in the palm of his hand.

"Where to?"

"Oh, just the common."

"But it's dark," said his mum.

"No it isn't, not properly. We won't be long."

"You sound as if you're up to something."

"It's just a game," said Adam quickly.

"I'll come with you," said his mum.

"Oh, let him go," said Dad. "He's got his friend – he'll be all right."

A rocket whooshed past the garden fence.

"Oooh," said Mum. "Look at that! They're setting off fireworks three weeks early – I bet you knew all the time! Can't we come and watch?"

"No!" shouted Adam. "Sorry, Mum, but – no."

He picked up Gary's coat.

"Off you go, then," said Dad. "Don't do anything daft."

Gary was swinging by his arms from a tree branch.

"Got your coat," said Adam briefly. Gary

dropped. “Come on. Let’s go.”

“Go where?”

“To the place, stupid.”

“But how are you going to find it?”

“Easy,” said Adam.

Gary sighed.

“OK,” he said. “You’re the boss.”

A few fences up, some people were setting off fireworks. Crimson and orange smoke hung in the air and kids ran about with sparklers. A wayward balloon sailed like a pale bubble past the dark trees.

Adam and Gary went the other way. It wasn’t a bit dark. Behind them they could hear the snap-fizz of another firework and all the kids squealing. The grey of the bushes was tipped with orange.

“Here,” he said. He heard his voice, sharp and bossy.

“Yes, sir,” teased Gary.

Adam took out the egg-thing, and carefully placed it among the ferns.

“Goodbye, bird,” he whispered.

"That all?" said Gary.

"Let's watch the fireworks," said Adam.

The grass was damp and prickly but they didn't care.

"Look at that one … ooooh! Three different colours."

"Pow! Pow-pow!" Gary machine-gunned the bangers.

"Wow! Look at that rocket! Brilliant! Hey – look! It's curving round! Watch it! It's going to land on — "

"Duck!"

A streak of brilliant light stabbed into the ground.

When they opened their eyes, everything was black.

In the distance, they could hear the kids oooohing and aaaahing.

Then all the colours came back, the russet and lavender smoke, the sudden biscuity brown of the ferns in a car's headlamps and the soft greeny greys of the trees.

Adam walked back to the place where he'd left the bird.

"Come and see."

Gary came running.

"Where is it?"

"It's gone," said Adam happily.

"Where?"

"Where it came from," said Adam.

Gary looked at him.

"You know, don't you?" he said respectfully.

"Well kind of..."

"Is it a strange planet? Does it have aliens on it?"

But the knowing was already fading.

"I can't remember."

"You mean, you won't."

"No I can't. Honest."

They began to walk back. Gary was thoughtful.

"That bird," he said. "Zoo couldn't have helped. Even my dad couldn't have helped. Did you see that rocket?"

"Course I did."

"Was it a spaceship, d'you think?" He snorted. "Little green men from Mars?"

"Dunno."

Gary spread out his fingers.

"Did they have tentacles? Slimy green tentacles? Tell me. Tell me!"

Adam was irritated.

"It was only a rocket," he said crossly. "Just one of their rockets... Look, there's another one!"

"But the bird was real."

"The bird was real."

"Then what happened?"

"Dunno."

Gary was silent for a bit.

"Hey, Adam..."

"What?"

"Are we nuts, d'you think?"

"Dunno."

"Loonies?"

Adam smiled. "Perhaps."

"It's gone."

"Yes."

"I got to go, too."

They walked back through the gate.

"Glad our lot don't do that, though," said Gary thoughtfully. "We never lost a pigeon yet. You ought to see our birds. They're not posh, like your one. But they're not bad. When you coming over?"

"Dunno."

"Monday? After school?"

"OK."

"See you, then."

"See you."